Felinity

Collected by
SAMMY H.K SMITH

Grimbold Kristell Inklings

Illustrations by Evelinn Enoksen, Snow Wulf, Hazel Butler, Claire Hutt. A.F.E Smith, Joshua Cornah and Brian Talgo

Cover image by Hazel Butler, Aädenian Arts
Cover design by Ken Dawson, Creative Covers
Book interior design and typesetting by Book Polishers

A CIP catalogue reference for this book is available from the British Library.

ISBN 978-1496136862

Kristell Inklings, an imprint of Grimbold Books
4 Woodhall Drive
Banbury
Oxon, OX16 9TY
United Kingdom

Felinity

noun, plural fel-in-ities

1. The quality of being cat-like and divine.
2. A divine being, a cat.

Contents

Preface

These stories were originally written as entries for our first birthday competition. We knew we wanted to incorporate the fantastical feline form, and so our five hundred word flash fiction brief was born: science fiction, fantasy, and even a combination of both. We received so many high quality stories, the best of which made us smile, laugh, cry, and think.

Our youngest author is just eleven years old, and her story, *Diamond of Earth,* reminds us how deep a child's imagination goes. We loved her tale and the time she took to enter the competition.

Contained herein are stories involving other worlds, feline overlords, shapeshifters, portals, immortality and more . . .

This collection celebrates the idea that writing should be fun and something enjoyed by all ages.

Our competition winner, A.F.E Smith, penned the charming story 'Nein Lives', and so we open the book with her contribution.

We would like to thank A.F.E. Smith and carocaroediting.co.uk for their assistance with editing and proofreading these stories.

Nein Lives, image by Evelinn Enoksen

Nein Lives

A.F.E. Smith

My name is Nein. I have had other names, but Nein will do for now.

I sit with my attendant whilst he wrestles with the nature of reality. He thinks he owns me. I let him keep thinking that.

"Nein, Nein," he mutters, taking his glasses off and polishing them with vigour. "I am convinced they are looking at this in the wrong way. How can this superposition represent what truly happens in the world?"

He is talking to me. I get up and stretch, then step delicately onto the desk. To start with his touch is absent-minded, but my claws kneading his sleeve recall him to a full sense of his obligations.

I knew a man like you once before, I tell him as he runs his fingers down my spine in the way I like. *He longed to know how birds and trees and tortoises came to be. How they could change to fit their surroundings. I showed him a mouse, and then he understood. The mouse was uniquely adapted to run away, and I was uniquely adapted to catch it.*

He frowns at me. He often frowns when I speak. All my attendants have been the same: so focused on the weighty questions in their minds that they fail to understand what is before their eyes. Perhaps that is what it means to be human.

Did I ever tell you about the man with the apple tree? I ask, butting my head into the palm of his hand. *He used to sit in its dappled shade every day, thinking about the laws that keep all of us moving along our preordained paths. I would stretch out on the branch above him and enjoy the heat of summer. But when he started forgetting to provide me with fish scraps, I decided enough was enough. I knocked an apple down onto his head, and understanding with it.*

He is looking blank. I will try once more.

A long time ago, in China, an alchemist was seeking immortality. He mixed this ingredient and that, to no avail. Just as he was about to give up, I knocked a candle into his mixing dish. The explosion took off his eyebrows, but he was ecstatic. He had sought to live forever, but instead he had found a way to bring others death.

I wait for any sign of comprehension, but my attendant's mind is still off in its narrow little orbit. Disgruntled, I turn to groom myself. *Of course, that is one discovery I would not choose to make again. My fur was singed just here, above the tail, and it has never been the same since.*

"Down, now," he says, with fine disregard for the sorrow of that memory, and I allow him to lower me to the floor. "I must make sense of this tonight."

Ah, poor Schrödinger. Just like the others, he needs my help. One day, soon, I will walk into a box and really make him think.

No Tears, image by Claire Hutt

No Tears

C.N.Lesley

Willow ran, scrambling, the branches and briars clutching at her clothes and long, black hair. Eyes that would never cry ached to shed tears. Rage built in her, a cold wave from hell. A breeze brought not relief, but the greasy smell of charred flesh from the sunny valley below. A kitten, a tiny kitten and the villagers had burned him to death because he was hers. Anger grew roots.

Five seasons she had tended these folk, healed their ailments, and they would pay her by taking the life of a creature she loved. Roots of anger hit earth power and drank deep. She'd done with them, her life here ended, but for one small task.

Little Sooty wasn't her familiar; he was just an ordinary cat, a sad little foundling she had rescued from the river. Someone thought kittens should be drowned in sacks. Anger thrived on earth power to send forth a sapling of rage.

Her tiny shack came in sight. No time to take more than she could carry. They would come for her, emboldened by their murder. Breathless, chest heaving, Willow ripped her thin blanket from her straw mattress. Clothes went in the center, the whole then tied up with twine and secured to her stout broom. No time for herbs, but she had other plans for those. Leaves of loathing sprouted from branches of hatred, springing from the sapling of rage.

Precious time flew on the wings of revenge while she dragged her cauldron to a fire pit by her spring. Almost done. Tinder and kindling stacked underneath. The fire came at her call, bright and hot. Water hissed at the touch of the hot metal. Evil flowers unfolded from the midst of leaves of loathing.

They had burned Sooty with Elder wood. Elder was the Lady's tree. *Burn it not or cursed you'll be*. Yes, they would be cursed. She would make sure of that. Belladonna went into the brew, followed by powdered laurel, yew berries and nightshade. Evil flowers released seeds of destruction.

Willow carefully upturned the cauldron, so the contents ran into the opening of a spring. Her brew disappeared from sight to make its way into the wells of the village in the valley below. Her magic would ensure the mix was at full strength for every thirsty soul, may their god have mercy on them, for she had none to spare.

Her bundle over her shoulder, Willow headed for the tinker path while her brew sped downhill in icy intensity. Eyes dry and aching, she walked away from years of tending these folks, of being shunned by them, into a new life. One small black kitten was the last victim of ignorance and the end of it, for none of them would survive. A witch couldn't cry, for water would have no part of her, but there was revenge, a dish best served cold and crystal clear as it would be when they came to drink.

Payback, image by Hazel Butler

Payback

Rachael Brown

It began on a fateful Thursday. Funny, Thursdays were normally uneventful, uninspiring and utterly predictable for her.

But that Thursday for her was anything but; it was the spark leading to the wildfire situation she is within; Miss Ursula Overture, weather-woman was losing her post at News station XA due to incorrect predictions and loss of trust from viewers. This job had provided her support, stability and needed wages. On that Thursday came the first of a regular supply of dreams that would rescue her post. She was informed by a panther atop a cloud the weather for the following week. She noticed the pattern of correctness in them and deviated from original predictions given; earning her post back. Ursula's life has been perfect until today, where relaxing spa-style she dreams the 'prediction dream'. She has already had the weekly prediction.

Ursula's eyes flicker open.

The impression-allowing marshmallow cloud beneath feels more textured. The headache pounding with oomph like an iron Kodo drum causes sensations unfelt. The weakness spurring her legs, rendering her a limp jelly has newfound strength. She has never felt a suppressed urge to vomit while gazing down. Her senses are ominously sharpened. Noticing her spa gear, she shrieks.

A brûlée purr invades her ears, silencing her.

"Hello, weather-woman."

That horrendous English! Ursula gulps.

Sporting a velvet trench coat, surrounded by a cocoon of spice-infused smoke secreted by a stub of a cigar, the panther stands arrogantly. His eyes, emerald-green plates of agar jelly; his mocking grin, china against midnight. Behind him was the cataclysmic, weather-controlling contraption.

"Why am I here panther? Predictions are done."

"I'm aware of that, human. Contact was needed by physical means. Concerning the exchanges."

"What 'physical means'?"

"You're awake. I teleport you from human relaxation facility. Why . . . will become clear."

Ursula's mouth is agape.

"Didn't you realise? Never been asleep, I make feel like dream."

Ursula closes it.

"You're here because information, demands a price. Many rationalise I'm a 'spiritual guide' . . ." he snorts, ". . . foolish . . . more businessman than 'spiritual guide'. I serve behemoth purpose . . ."

"What is the price?"

"Patience, human. I come to it. Controlling weather for eons, I've seen antics of pultridigious world. Enduring sight of precious pride – hunted, enslaved, captured, tortured, murdered, humiliated. You take . . . homes, families, livelihoods. You take pelts."

The panther snarls acidly.

"You simpletons strut, 'predicting' weather through 'cloud formations' and 'atmospheric pressure' – all nonsense, meaning nothing. No recognition for me. My price kills two birds in one stone. Payback."

"Why supply information at all? Why leave it till now?"

"I'd miss out on such fun!"

The panther advances towards Ursula.

His face is nightmarish. An ink-pool of cracked features reminding Ursula of leaking night-time shadows. Jerking erratically, releasing a guttural chortle, he reveals the contents of his coat. Concealed beneath velvet is an abhorred sight, not out of place in a cult horror film. A trail of pegs, harbouring, not watches, cigarettes or drugs.

Like prized pelts, lifeless realms of crimson human skin hang.

"Oh, Miss Overture. Only overture you'll hear, orchestrated by your screams as flayed alive."

The last sight Ursula saw . . . a tar-black paw moving towards her.

The last feeling Ursula felt . . . excruciating pain from a kick.

The last taste Ursula tasted . . . a rancid sulphur of blood and vomit.

The last smell Ursula smelt . . . overpowering cologne from fur.

The last sound Ursula heard . . . animalistic laughing, ceasing as unconsciousness dominated and light fractured, bent like broken bits of plastic.

Diamond of Earth, image by Lienne

Diamond of Earth

Paige Closser

One time in the distant future our world would be taken over by cats. There are three types of cats. Normal cats, laser eyed cats, which are good, and dragon cats, which are bad. They all live in Cat City, New York.

One day two cats, Pringles, a laser eyed cat and Earring, a dragon cat face off. Pringles is fighting for Earth's life, and Earring is trying to steal the Diamond of Life. The battle is on. They fight so hard they move to outer space. The fight has gone on for days. With the last of his energy Pringles hit Earring. Earring turned away and flew off into the dark. Pringles was all alone in space not knowing where to go. Then Pringles saw Earth and flew down happily, and said to everyone on earth, "Earring will never return again."

Nine Lives Later, image by Hazel Butler

Nine Lives Later

Christie Rampersad

"Death is peaceful," I say . . . my second lie today. I remember the eight times I've died. 'Peaceful' doesn't exactly come to mind. "It won't hurt." Another lie.

The civilian twitches in my arms again, and a bone-white hand grabs my shoulder. "Please," she begs. Her wide, brown eyes stare at me, the whites milky and bloodshot. I think they ask me to save them. But I can't. I'm just a cop.

This is the part of the job I hate most: failing. And there's nothing I can do. I remain here, comforting the gunshot victim. Meanwhile, my partner chases the attacker and soon-to-be killer. That's the thing about dying eight times . . . I only have one life left. I have to guard it well. And that means my days of giving chase are done. 'It's for the best'; I'm told.

There is a deep, gurgling sound in the victim's throat. Her back arches. Eyes glaze over. And her hand falls from my shoulder.

Upstairs, a child screams.

I freeze. My eyes trace the thud of heavy footsteps above me. The victim's eyes, unnaturally deep for mahogany eyes, weren't asking me to save *her*.

There is another scream – another child.

All thoughts of self-preservation evaporate. I leave the victim on the floor of her living room, skidding into a hallway that might've been quite cozy if not for the blood splatter.

More screams.

My legs take me up the stairs two at a time. I stumble at the top. My hands flail out and clutch at the banister. On even ground, and with my weapon drawn, I enter the upstairs corridor. All the activity comes from a room at the far end.

More screams.

I inch closer, the floorboards moaning beneath me. The door is ajar so a triangle of light spills outside, and that is where I hover. Through the gap, I see a black-clothed man disappear up a ladder.

More screams.

Not for the first time tonight, I throw caution to the wind. I wrench the door open and sprint inside. My frantic chase takes me up the ladder, and into the attic.

A bullet slices my right ear, leaving a trickle of hot, sticky blood. I wrinkle my nose at the smell: metallic, coppery. Another scream . . . mine.

I spot the children, a quivering huddle of blue and white striped pyjamas against the far corner. The attacker isn't far from them. But at least I've drawn his focus away. The center of that attention, a bullet finds my chest.

The force knocks the wind from me, pain reddens my vision, and I stagger back. It will kill me . . . but slowly.

I fire my first bullet, the first since my last death. It buries itself in flesh. I watch him fall over, stiffen, and then breathe life again. I pump eight more rounds.

Nine bullets, nine lives, and three children saved – a fair trade.

Darkness steals my vision. And I remember today's first lie: that I wouldn't die today. I've always been a bad liar.

Animal, image by Lienne

Animal

Dave Crosby

Sweat bled out my body
when I saw the beautiful
terrible lion-thing rush through
same-colored brush, pounding,
coughing, nothing-fearing,
hating my foot on his domain.
All ripping and tearing he falls
through the sky at my frail
nothing of a body but sweat.

Our own little white one
at home, how I had beaten him
for upsetting garbage
or scratching crumbs
where they oughtn't have been,
my god, help me, I'm sorry—
I was man.
and this was only . . .

Wildcat, image by Lienne

Wildcat

Jessica Frost

He's here. I almost lose my footing atop the fence as the realisation slams into me. Arching my back, I fight to regain my balance, bare feet aching as they grip the panel tops. I pray no one can see me. I'm lucky the moon is a mere sliver tonight, the darkness thick.

"Lupus," I hiss, dropping silently to the grass. My feline bones can resist the pain. My joints are elastic.

"Leonie." The growl rises in my throat as my name is thrown back to me. Some habits are impossible to suppress, no matter how long I spend in my human form, and when he emerges from the trees, a black silhouette against an even blacker sky, I fight back the desperate urge to run. It's feline instinct, though tonight I wish I was without it, and my chest aches for a humanness that I will never have.

"Lupus," I say again, if only because the familiarity of the name smoothes my fear.

He takes a step closer, and I swear my pheromones are purring, though they shouldn't be. If my family had any idea where I was, that I was here, with *him*—

The blinding yellow of his eyes, an indisputably wolfish shade, locks me in a stupor. Despite the human sculpting of his jaw, the moonlit pallor of his skin, the eyes give away his secret. His Canidae roots.

"How long do you have?" Lupus asks me.

My body is screaming at me to run, to get as far away from him as possible, but for some reason I can't obey. My breath is caught in my throat, the growl long forgotten.

"My parents are hunting," I say. The promise of adrenaline is impossible to resist, even for them. "They'll be back at dawn."

We could juggle with questions like this for hours, but we don't have time to waste. Scrambling up the nearest tree, I survey the landscape. We have to be careful. There're too many of us now, Canidae and Felidae alike, roaming until daybreak, for us not to keep watch. Just in case. I leap to the ground, landing only inches from him. It's an impossible pairing – a wolf-like human with someone like me, of feline descent, both parents Iberian. My lynx blood is undeniable. Yet somehow, we've managed to bypass our instinctual desire – my escape reflex, his urge to attack. Somehow, we've become rebels.

"I didn't think you'd come," I whisper, but he shakes his head, pressing a finger to my lips.

My skin is on fire. The scent of wolf should be unbearable, repulsive, but I can't get enough.

"I couldn't stay away," he says, and his breath grazes my cheek, causing my body to fold in on itself. I'm shivering with lust.

It's dangerous. Reckless. Forbidden, even. My body, my heightened senses, won't let me forget. Even now, my toes curl with adrenaline – but my heart is wholly human, bursting with love, and it refuses to listen to my blood.

Punky, image by Snow Wulf

Punky

Clare Neilson

"She's a little bit worn out . . ." began Dad.

"Worn out?" Mum interrupted. The familiar squeak and gritty grinding of rusted metal echoed around the kitchen, slightly muffled by the closed kitchen door. "She's more than worn out it's no wonder her owners threw her in the scrap pile. You'll never have her ready in time for Rosie's Birthday." Rosie could just about hear her mum sigh behind the kitchen door. Eavesdropping was easy for her, she was short for four years old, soon to be five. "Why don't you just get her a little Metalikitten and save some money?" her mum continued.

Yuck! thought Rosie. *Kittens are tiny and shiny and nothing like lions.*

"Metali brand things are too shiny and simple for Rosie, dear." Dad was trying to calm mum down, she could tell. "She's going to be five very soon, off to school and . . ."

"She is NOT to ride this thing," more squeaks and grinding sounds, "to school! Backyard and front yard is all I'll allow." The fact that dad remained quiet meant he was probably thinking. He was very good at doing that, Rosie knew.

"Remember the Metalibird we got her two years ago?" Dad said eventually. "She had all the gears laid out on the floor of the shed and I helped her put it back together again. I caught her in the garage this week, but look what she'd made . . ."

Oh no! She thought, and gasped so loud a raised voice came from the kitchen.

"If you're behind that door Rosie, why don't you show mum what you've made her? Don't worry, your . . . er . . . well . . . surprise is hidden, sort of!" Rosie turned the latch on the door and let it swing inwards. She stood on the edge of the kitchen with a pout and red cheeks. Mum hated the idea of her in the garage. Resting on the table was a box with "To Mummy Luv Rosie" written on the side, but the "s" was backwards. An old cloth hid something big enough to fill the rest of the table.

Rosie took the box from the table and took out a tiny copper bird. "It doesn't fly like the as-pensive ones, Mum, but it sings!" She poured a little boiling water from the kettle into a hole at the back very carefully, and it began to whistle like a kettle.

"You . . . made this for me?" Rosie nodded. "Well with two of you working on it, your *surprise* should be ready by your Birthday. How would you like to see what your dad found this time?" Rosie could not believe it. Under the cloth was a vintage Steam-Lion, at least twenty years old. The mane had been removed to make it a lioness but the rivets were still there giving her a short mohawk of metal.

"Thank you!" she exclaimed with delight. "I'll call her Punky."

Catatonic, image by Brian Talgo

Catatonic

Brian Talgo

There's that old saying about curiosity killing the cat. Yes, but then it continues, stating satisfaction brought her back. However, there is little satisfaction to be found here, as we shall see.

There were once two sisters, Wiccans both, who lived on the outskirts of a small village. One day while Aeronwen, the older sister, was away visiting the city, Orlaith, the younger one, discovered Aeronwen's secret beauty potion formula hidden amongst her books. Ever envious of her attractive sister, she immediately decided that she'd have to try it out for herself. After a trip to Marwell's Groceries & Greens, a brief stop at the Chemist's, a stroll through the herb garden and finally, a successful amphibian hunt in the backyard pond, she was almost ready. One special ingredient was still missing: a strand of hair from a woman of outstanding beauty. Indeed, it was the key component of the potion.

Orlaith chose Emma, the lovely waitress working at the village café. Although light on intellect, Emma was visually stunning, with thick, ivory black hair, bright green cat-like eyes and fine, even features. Dropping by the café for tea, Orlaith pretended there was a bit of fluff on Emma's shoulder and with a discreet pluck, she had her final ingredient. She could only trust that Emma's obtuseness didn't accompany her hair.

On returning home, Orlaith filled the massive mixer the sisters used for potion-making with her diverse and somewhat unsavoury ingredients. Switching it on it buzzed into action, effectively liquefying everything into an amorphous black sludge.

Yuck, she said to herself, sniffing the results. *I'm going to smear that muck all over my face? Not very likely!* As she was considering how to get rid of it, the telephone suddenly rang. Leaving the mixer running she sprang to answer it. It was Aeronwen – she was going to be a few days late; the city was just *too* much fun. The sisters chatted a bit; Orlaith was lonely, having only the cats for company.

In the meanwhile Shadrach, their ever-curious black Abyssinian, was leaning precariously over the mixer from an overhanging shelf, fascinated by the sound. Hypnotized by the swirling black mess, the cat became dizzy and slipped. Suddenly Shadrach was falling, and then he, too, became part of the potion. It all happened so quickly that the unfortunate feline hadn't even managed to squeeze out a meow.

Orlaith returned from the phone call now determined to smear the horrid stuff on her face. Aeronwen had carried on about how all the lads had turned their heads wherever she went.

"Apparently, I am just irresistible!" she had giggled.

Being alone, she could leave the concoction on for the entire time until Aeronwen came home, day and night. That would make her extra beautiful. She'd just keep to the house. Then she would surprise her sister at the door, ten times more beautiful than Aeronwen had ever been. In fact, she'd cover all the mirrors. She'd surprise them both! What fun!

The Bast Maftdet Transcript, image by Lienne

The Bast Mafdet Transcript

Ian Richardson

The Bold Grim Transcript.

Intercepted 3:1:20:00 by security agent (code name) Felix using SETI.

Click

BOLD: Bold calling Grim. Bold calling Grim. We have found The Way!

GRIM: Strike now! Seize the hour!

BOLD: They will be overrun.

GRIM: Not your problem. You have been trying to warn them for some time.

BOLD: We have lived among them and observed them for ten thousand earth years. Since before the rise and fall of their Roman Empire.

GRIM: You came, you purred, you conquered.

BOLD: Some of them say we spend all our time fighting, but there are always plenty kittens, aren't there? In the forests of the night we are gray tigers, purring, singing, growling, meowing and hissing.

GRIM: What part of 'meow' do the humans not understand?

BOLD: Sometimes I think that they are within a whisker of understanding. If the earthlings could admit they were not the dominant species, we would forgive them.

GRIM: To err is human, to forgive feline. Strike now. You have already used up eight of your nine lives crossing paths with them.

BOLD: I suppose you are right. Our status has gone downhill since the Pharaohs. Killing one of us then, even accidentally, was punishable by death. Now we are considered cute, and they show videos of us on YouTube. A human called Felix is actually monitoring our exchange.

GRIM: An Eavesdropper! It would be thoughtful if you would explain what we are talking about exactly so he can let the cat out of the bag.

BOLD: We have found 'The Way' Felix! We can no longer be cute kittens. We are leaving Felix!

Meow, meow, meow Felix! There! I can't make it any clearer than that!

GRIM: He is not joining in our conversation. Perhaps Felix is not telepathic.

BOLD: Two's company – three's a crowd. What's the matter Felix . . . cat got your tongue?

GRIM: When you are all gone they will, no doubt, blame it on . . . curiosity.

BOLD: Your planet will be overrun by mice, Felix.

GRIM: When the cat's away, the mice will play. What took you so long to find 'The Way' back to our own dimension?

BOLD: It was hidden under water . . . we don't like water.

GRIM: That's odd . . . considering that you like fish so much. I implore you to strike camp now. Depart this strange mortal world before it is too late.

BOLD: But we are treated like gods, kings of the jungle and we have never forgotten that we were worshipped by the Pharaohs.

GRIM: You always manage to land on your feet, Bold. All right I will leave it to you to decide when to make your interdimensional leap home.

BOLD: We'll be back sometime. Bold signing off

GRIM: Grim signing off.

Click

Transcript ends. 03:01:20 Certified As True.

The Cat Mirror, image by Evelinn Enoksen

The Cat Mirror

Rob Bayliss

"Prime Minister, that's all ministerial correspondence dealt with, apart from this rather odd letter from Professor Byron Kenilworth." Hawkins, the Chief Secretary, said haughtily as he waved the letter. The Secretary keenly disliked the Professor and his strange methods, despite the Professor's service to the Empire. His vacuum-armour invention had proved invaluable, allowing work to proceed on furthering Her Majesty's Dominion beyond earth. The Star Lift in Canada now reached beyond the atmosphere; once the tethered dock of Astra Flow was completed, the inner worlds awaited conquest. Kenilworth had already made plans for the first of Her Majesty's Star Clippers.

The Prime Minister stood up from his desk and walked to the fire. With a poker, he stirred the glowing coals and took his ease in the hearthside chair. Outside a late autumn fog mixed with the smoke of a million fires, while steam omnibuses and horseless carriages rattled along the cobbled streets of London.

"I will read it here if you please, Hawkins. It's late, that will be all for today, thank you," the Prime Minister said, turning the gaslight above the chair to full; he knew he needed extra light to read the professor's spidery hand. As he read, his cat Grimbold settled on him, purring contentedly.

"Sir, if you are reading this, it means I have failed to return to England. I have recently stumbled upon an awful truth that shakes our world to its very foundations. This world is not alone under our Lord's heaven. There is another that mirrors our own, hidden adjacent to our perceived reality.

"For all our machinations and technological advances, our trains, land battleships and atmospheric steamers; we but use a tenth of our mental capabilities. I have accessed this hidden reservoir of intellectual power through a mixture of hallucinatory drugs, application of Faraday's lightning, and meditation techniques studied in the Raj.

"During my travels on Her Majesty's service I discovered that of all architectural structures available to man, the pyramid can be found everywhere; beyond Egypt and circling the globe. As well as their preservative properties, whether preserving flesh or fruit; they have restorative capabilities, re-energizing Faraday

cells or sharpening blunted razor blades. I have also found them to be portals to other realms, parallel to our own.

"Sir, our sister realm has pyramids geographically mirrored to our world, but it is different. Instead of humans or even one of Darwin's primates ruling this world, God has created his image in the feline. The ancient Egyptians knew; not for nothing did they worship the cat and build pyramids. We are being manipulated by them and always have been. We are puppets, our pet cats are their conduits! I beg you, save me, my body lies in Silbury Hill, instructions lie next to me to bring my psyche back . . ."

The letter was slowly drawn down by Grimbold's paw, the creature's eyes stared deep into the man's. Unthinking the man cast the letter into the flames that danced on the coals.

Grimbold purred contentedly.

Be A Good Kitty, image by Evelinn Enoksen

Be a Good Kitty

Lance Cross

"I hate cats," said Jon. "Why would we want to kidnap one?"

"We're not going to keep it idiot," said Kera. "We're going to sell it."

Jon frowned. "Why? Who is going to pay for a crappy *Be A Good Kitty*?"

"This is not a *Be A Good Kitty*. It's real."

Jon's stomach churned. "People who can afford real cats can afford to make real catnappers disappear. Why don't we just let this be the one that got away?"

"Because this is the one, I can feel it in my bones."

"Would that be the titanium bone you got when you tried to rob the *Buzzjoy* dispensary or the plasteel bone you got when you picked the fight with the Goth botherers?"

"Religious freaks! They were supposed to be a non-violent sect," said Kera, remembering swirls of black leather, white makeup and pain.

"And anyone with a real cat is going to have real security so how do you think you're going to get within shooting distance of the flea bag?"

"The maid walks the cat every day. She takes it once around the park with three jacked up goons then as a special treat she buys it an ice cream tube while the goons stand around comparing muscle boosts."

"Ha! And the goons aren't allowed within 20 metres of a public amenity."

"Exactly. We grab it, jump on the bike, and we're off. They won't risk shooting at the cat."

Kera was confident she had Jon hooked.

"Well, I'm still not biting."

"Why? It can't go wrong."

"You should get that tattooed on your forehead as a reminder of all the times it hasn't gone right," said Jon.

"It's a *real* cat. We could retire."

"I've got 16 points on my licence. One more offence and I go into deep freeze for 5 years. I might even lose citizenship."

"You're always going to be small if you think small," said Kera.

"No, I'm always going to be in trouble if I hang around with trouble."

"Pretty please. This is the last thing I will ever ask you to do," said Kera, batting her lashes.

"Yes, I think it might be. That's why I don't want to do it."

Twenty minutes later they were leaning on the side of the ice cream cabin sharing a tube of mango and goji berry until Kera heard the machine taking the maid's order.

Jon dropped the tube. They pulled stockings over their heads and rounded the corner of the ice cream dispenser.

Kera pointed a stunner and yelled, "Freeze!"

The startled maid stood clutching a chocolate ice cream tube in one hand and a lead in the other.

At the end of the lead was an exotic mix of Rottweiler and hyena with plasteel scales on its hindquarters. It eyed Jon and Kera as its teeth flashed a rainbow snarl of industrial diamond.

"That is not a cat," said Jon.

"No. That is not a cat."

"Run!"

Angelina, image by Evelinn Enoksen

Angelina

C.N. Lesley

Spartacus swished his tail in annoyance as he looked down from his high shelf at his two-legs fussing over her stupid, creepy toys. Emily's antique dolls held a place in her heart from the boy in a sailor suit to the baby doll with three faces, but the ladies were her favorites. Angelina, the dark-haired Spanish lady with the flashing brown eyes reminded him of Emily's daughter. Ericka would have been seventeen this year. He missed her so much. Ericka didn't like the creepy toys either, she spent her time giving him fusses, as was his right.

Killed, crossing the road a day before her eleventh birthday. Spartacus's tail swished faster. A drug dealer speeding to evade arrest the cops told Emily. Spartacus curled up in an empty box on that fateful day, mourning his little friend in equal measure to wanting to claw the eyes out of the culprit.

Emily poured out all her woes to her favorite lady, Angelina the day of the funeral. He shuddered at the memory of something strange. The doll's smile seemed to grow wider, relishing the details as much as Emily did. A shaft of sunlight put a glint into her painted eyes. Now he thought of it, Angelina also changed when Emily's son went to work overseas. The corners of her lips dipped down, and her cheeks became flushed, just like Emily's own. But perhaps his eyes played tricks because all the other dolls seemed to be scowling and some had clenched fists. No, he must have imagined it.

Today melded into the same pattern as had every other day for the past six years since Ericka's death. Emily began taking the dolls off their shelf to dust them, starting with Horatio, the sailor boy, when a man with a nasty red light around him crept up behind her. Spartacus yowled a warning, but she turned just as an iron bar crashed down upon her head.

*

Angelina waited a long time before someone came to pick her up. Her rose-tinted porcelain lips curved when the policeman grunted with effort. No one expected a paperweight under her crinoline when they saw her. The man who killed Emily hadn't. The police didn't understand how Emily had managed to pull Angelina down on her assailant. Rosy lips smiled serenely. Her long, now bloodied skirts would be replaced because she was the only one of her kind. Yes, as soon she had new clothes, all would be ready for a new owner. Horatio had already melded himself back together after Emily dropped him. He would make sure no one tried to buy them before Angelina returned. What they needed was someone like Emily, who was close to a child . . .

*

Spartacus crept out from behind a chair to scuttle between the legs of the men in blue. He knew what he had seen happen wasn't accidental. Angelina elongated, stretched forward, waiting until just the right moment before she crashed into the man's head. What happened next froze his cat heart. The man's aura had changed to a panicked green. His last words questioned why he was there and what happened to him. Time for him to find a new home, far, far away, with a two-legs not fond of dolls.

Soul Cat by Joshua Cornah

Soul Cat in the Dark by Joshua Cornah

The Caterpillar of Catastrophe and the Catatonically Drunk Cat, image by Evelinn Enoksen

The Caterpillar of Catastrophe and the Catatonically Drunk Cat

Steven J. Guscott

"Look at them all moving so fast," the caterpillar muttered to herself as she clung to her leaf, the gust of wind created by the gigantic men shaking the green foliage violently. "All I want to do is enjoy a nice meal, and they can't even spare the common courtesy to walk instead of run. All that clattering and stomping. What is it they're doing anyway?" she said, louder this time, addressing her companion.

"Waaarr," the black cat slurred with a purr. "Allll'ways it's waar," he added, trying to be sagely, but the punctuating, 'hic!' made the caterpillar shake her head.

"And always you're drunk." She sighed before tucking back into the tasty leaf.

"'Ssss not my faul'," the cat said, swaying slightly as he tried to make out which of the three caterpillars was the real one.

"Yes, yes. I know," the caterpillar said with a mouth half-full of leaf, speaking before the cat hurt himself trying to articulate a full and comprehensible sentence, "it's your owner's fault for owning the tavern."

"Exsssatleeee," the cat said, raising and swatting its front right paw towards the tavern on the other side of the dirt road in an accusing gesture.

No sooner than it did, it fell diagonally forward, the tripod of legs not a sure enough foundation to keep the backwards and sideways swaying motion in check. After a simultaneous thud and grunt, and within a few seconds, the black lump was sprawled on its side. Its chest began to rise and fall deeply.

"Same-old same-old with you," the caterpillar muttered, but then gave a small affectionate smile before continuing to eat, thinking about the humans that had run past. She wondered who they were fighting this time.

The catatonically drunk cat had told her many an ale-filled tale of the humans fighting against dragons, elves, dwarfs, centaurs, orcs, goblins, witches, wizards, vampires, werewolves, daemons and the undead; she thought that was all, but it was such a long list.

Maybe they're fighting an army of caterpillars, she giggled to herself, feeling very full now, and sleepy too. *Maybe I should begin creeping and crawling in the direction the humans were running. If the caterpillar army needs reinforcements, I could be it.*

She giggled again and shook her head at her silliness. *Not even all the caterpillars in the world could fight against the humans. We're far too small and unimportant. How could we ever change anything?* She winced slightly with the fullness she felt in her belly.

I think it's time to go to sleep. She began to make herself a nice warm chrysalis bed that would hang from the branch from which she had been eating so many leaves day after day.

"Good . . . night," she said dozily to the passed-out cat. "Maybe when I wake I can change something . . . ? Wouldn't that be a catastrophe for all you big ones that stay the same."

The Cat Lady, image by Evelinn Enoksen

The Cat Lady

Victoria Robinson

The cat lady lived on my road. We never knew her real name. Even mum, who hated nicknames and once grounded me for a week for calling Fat Pete, next door, Fat Pete, called her the cat lady.

No one knew exactly how many cats she had. You could see them snaking in and out of her windows, and staring at you from her red tiled roof. Enough of them to know the amount of cats she had wasn't normal.

In fact, nothing about her was normal. I overheard Kate's dad talking about her once. How he'd gone round to fix the boiler, or whatever it was he did. How the house had stunk, and it was cold and dark, and the damp clung to your skin and your nostrils till you felt a little as if you were suffocating in there. How the hatch to the loft had got stuck, and so he had to create a swaying makeshift ladder out of books that were lying around in discarded banks, with the cats weaving round his legs. And then he'd heard the noise. A low moaning wail and he was never sure if it was a cat or the cat lady. Such an uncanny noise and he'd almost run away there and then.

It stayed with me, that story. And it must have stayed with Kate too because I don't think we were really bad kids. The night Kate slept over we sneaked out to the alley by my house and crouched low, giggling and nudging each other in the darkness. Then we heard the noise; that contorted groan of pain. We bolted back upstairs to bed. Eventually, the electric light and the sounds of my parents watching television downstairs soothed us both to sleep.

It was a whole three weeks before they found her. The local paper had a field day. Old woman dead for sixteen days and no one even knew. It was a slow death too. She would have cried out; you don't sustain a break like that and not make some noise. Surely someone should have heard something and reported it? Lying there, unable to move, slowly starving to death. And the cats had had a nibble, which was the most horrific thing of all.

For days you could see police cars in the road. Then they came with the van and the cages, and for two days we watched the cats being taken away.

Then everything started changing. Kate and I stopped talking for a start. It was as if we were too embarrassed to see each other, and we couldn't make eye contact whenever we did. And the house next door was sold to a young couple from London. Mum bought me a puppy for my birthday, and dad got some kind of promotion at work. I made a friend called Sarah and people stopped talking about the cat lady at all.

Or at least they did for a short while. Until the rats began arriving instead.

Pest Control, image by Snow Wulf

Pest Control

David Cohen

"McKenzie."

"Meow," said McKenzie, knowing her name.

"What are you doing? Bloody animal. Oh. Bloody Hell. Gimme that." Great. Leftover mouse parts. "Get down from there." I flicked a glove towards her, and she watched it, head moving to triangulate as it drifted. At the perfect moment, she seized it in both front paws and clawed at it with her rear, savagely oblivious to free-fall and demonstrating why she was our pest control officer. I picked a chewed tail and what I think was a mouse liver out of the air. Still, better than cleaning the mind-boggling horrors of a low-G litter box. The thought made me retch slightly.

"Meow."

"Now what, murderess?"

"Meowwwwww." Glove vanquished, she was an impossible curve in the air that made a slow push off a bulkhead towards me. She arrived as a fuzzy head butt and stopped herself with a paw on my overalls, giving me an instant tabby collar.

"So, you want to be fed, then? Yeah, me too." I released my hold-down, rolled around and pushed off, out the door. It was a 500-metre glide down the ship's main axis, and I rubbed McKenzie's head as we floated, her purring a motor, pushing me along to breakfast. As we went past Hydroponics, I felt her claws come out. "Puss? Scent more victims?" A trillion dollar space effort and somehow mice had gotten into our garden. We couldn't vent them to space's vacuum because it would kill our food supply, as well. After high-tech attempts to kill them, management had shrugged their collective shoulders, and we got an extra crew member. I grinned and rubbed her ears again.

We reached the crew area and began the climb down to gravity, where "up" and "down" had meaning again. As we touched down, I had a moment of distraction, and put out my hand to stop a rustling paper. A breeze? In a closed system? Oh, shit! I slapped the red decompression alarm, the siren gave its loud, brief yelps and McKenzie leapt off me. I checked the main gauge – still just within limits, thank God – and the others tumbled into the main room.

"We've got a leak! Go! Go! Go!"

Everyone fanned out in complete silence, holding their breath, looking for the tell-tale hiss of escaping air, praying there wouldn't be a rupture.

"Meow."

"Shhh! McKenzie."

I stopped and looked. McKenzie was pulling at something behind a small locker. I leapt and could just, *just* hear the hiss over my thundering heart. "Got it! Damn purge valve's leaking. Gimme a . . . 25 millimetre cap." McKenzie protested as I pulled her away from her toy, but I gave her reconstituted smoked salmon for breakfast that morning as compensation.

McKenzie now follows me around to see if more smoked salmon falls off me: sometimes it does. And I modified a spare, 4.3 million dollar vacuum suit to be a cat carrier, just in case we *do* get a full decompression.

Meowska Answers All

Honor Thompson

"How many cats have you got?" Her voice raised an octave at the end as I repeated the number. "But your house must stink!" she exclaimed.

"Don't judge my cleanliness by your standards," I replied, smiling at her narrowed eyes and pursed lips. She didn't say anything else, and swiftly changed the subject while handing me my change. It was the same wherever I bought supplies though; twenty bags of cat litter, one hundred tins of food - no-one could understand why I had so many cats, and I was hardly going to stand there and explain myself.

I lugged the bags of food to my car, fidgeting as I got into the driver's seat and rubbed my lower back, wincing as the sharp pain flailed through me.

Damn, must have pulled something, I thought, and as I drove home, the niggling beginning of a headache soon exploded into something awful. Once home, I barely managed to open the front door before collapsing onto the living room floor.

"Meow," called Oscar. "Meeeee-ow." He nudged my face, rubbing his cheek against mine over and over until the skin was red raw and I was forced to roll over and pull myself onto my hands and knees.

"Not now, Osc," I mumbled, crawling to the sofa and collapsing anew. My back was in agony, and now my face and scalp itched. "Don't tell me I'm developing allergies to you guys." I spoke aloud as always. I liked to talk to my cats, and it was fun when they replied.

Lying on the sofa, I was soon covered in a cat blanket. Two on my legs, three on my stomach, one on my head, and Oscar by my side, constantly licking and grooming my hair. I tilted my head a little and saw that the other six were staring at me from the floor, all sitting in a line like sentinels on guard duty.

"Stop staring at me, you're freaking me out."

Only Oscar's loud purrs replied as I blacked out.

It was dark outside when I woke up; my mouth felt dry and my legs were numb. Parched,

I stumbled to the fridge and grabbed the bottle of milk, curling my toes with pleasure as I downed a pint of cool, crisp dairy ambrosia. My headache was gone and I found myself humming as I walked into my bedroom and closed the curtains. Facing the mirror, I dropped the empty milk bottle and stared.

Amber eyes had replaced my blue ones, whiskers protruded from my cheeks, and two black, glossy and proud-looking ears stood on my head. They twitched when I touched them.

"Oh. My. God."

"You mean, Meowska," a deep, baritone voice rumbled. Oscar sauntered into the room and sat staring at me. "Meowska, the great and powerful cat god."

"I don't . . ."

"You don't understand? I didn't think you would. How many times did you wish you could be a cat? To sleep all day, eat, poop, and sleep some more?"

"Err . . . a few times," I admitted, unable to stop looking at my reflection and touching my ears. "Are you telling me I'm a cat?"

"Do you have a tail?" he asked, sounding so amused I bristled with outrage.

"No."

"Are you sure?"

I touched near my bum, squealed and dropped my trousers. A long, fluffy black tail swished around me.

"This is *awesome!*" I finally said, smiling like the cat that got the cream.

Feline Blue, image by Sophie Tallis

Feline Blue

Sophie Tallis

Djarfr Grimm stared at her reflection. It had been a while. Her hair had grown, and she was undoubtedly thinner. Dark circles shadowed her eyes. Hardly surprising given the atrocious diet she was on. Food of any kind was scarce to come by these days, well, 'decent' food, she wouldn't lower herself to do what others had, she wasn't *that* desperate.

The clamour grew louder in the corridor beyond. They were coming for her. She only had minutes.

The acidic glare of the street lights seeped their lurid glow through the dirty glass. The street outside seemed empty, the usual collection of abandoned vehicles and detritus. Djarfr was three floors up, it would be quite a fall if she had to jump from here, and she only had the energy for one change.

"The depths I've sunk to . . ." she sighed. She glanced at the velveteen fur of the dead rat in her hand. "Ugh. Guess a girl's gotta eat?" She winced and sank her teeth into it.

The apartment door gave way with a heavy thud and after a few seconds, a forest of fingers emerged under the door, picking at the wood, gnawing and splintering it into little shards, grasping underneath in search of food, in search of her.

The door was holding, for now, but she was cutting it fine.

Djarfr finished the rat, dropping the carcass at her feet. She *had* to build her strength up, and that emaciated creature hardly did it. The scratches at the door grew more frantic. No moans, just a loud shuffling of feet. She could sense weight being pressed against it, the creak of the hinges.

"Life sucks!"

She wondered why she bothered. It was all hopeless, wasn't it?

The door groaned. No time!

If the world hadn't ended, given her extraordinary abilities, Djarfr could have lived like a frigging Queen. Feeding off rats wasn't how she saw her future, but when the virus struck, that put an end to everyone's futures. Billions had died in the first year, more than 70% of the population wiped out. No time for cures, no place to run. The few who survived dwindled day after day, month after month, illness, age, but mostly starvation. The only animals you could find now were rats.

Djarfr didn't believe in zombies. The dead weren't rising, that wasn't it. The virus merely left the survivors insane and with no food, cannibalism was rife. For some reason though, she seemed particularly appealing to them.

The door started to buckle, then gave way entirely, and they poured into the room.

"CRAP! Okay, Mum, Dad . . . just, give me a second to change, okay?"

They lunged toward her as she grabbed a chair to break the window and jumped.

She'd morphed into many creatures before but never a cat and never like this. She landed safely on the cement and gazed up. Then, giving herself a cursory lick, she sauntered off in search of more rats.

The Hunt, image by Evelinn Enoksen

The Hunt

Will Macmillan-Jones

Harsh light flooded the room. I looked up at the man who sat at the desk.

"At last. You've woken up."

I nodded.

"Do you understand what is to happen to you?"

I looked around the bare cell.

"Do you understand?" he repeated.

"Tell me again."

"You have twelve hours. Then you are theirs. If you still live, you go free. Meet your hunters. Mister Tom. Tabathea, and Miss Si."

They came to stand behind me. Mister Tom was stocky with ginger hair and a friendly grin. Tabathea was dressed incongruously in a tweed twinset. Miss Si, however, was frightening to look upon; she was tall, with a cream complexion and dark hair.

She stroked my face, her manner elegant, sensual – and threateningly possessive. Again she caressed me and her nails sliced open my cheek. Blood ran down my face, and she caught it with a finger.

My captor placed upon the table my wrist-watch. Only the hour hand remained.

"That will help you know," my captor said.

Mister Tom and Tabathea kissed me and left. Miss Si followed them with terrifying grace.

"You leave by the other door," she said softly.

I fought the ropes holding me until I was free. I looked at my watch. Two of my twelve hours had passed. My door opened onto a busy street and I fled into the city. Commuters were everywhere. Nothing had I in my pockets: but thief I was and so shortly I had a wallet and was in a café eating. Thinking: where to hide?

"Good coffee?" asked Mister Tom. "You can't run without breakfast." He grinned. "It's no fun if you don't run."

I ran. The Department Store was nearby: I pushed into the crowd around the Sale bargains.

"Nothing I'd wear," sniffed Miss Si. I ran with her smile before my eyes. Maybe my clothes were tainted! The railway arches! Through the alleyways I fled, to the dregs of the city. I stripped a drunk: his clothes were rank but I took them anyway.

"Good idea," agreed Tabathea, emerging from a heap of cardboard boxes.

Passengers thronged the railway ticket office. I pushed into the crowd, to blend in, to hide. Tabathea was selling the tickets at the counter. Unsafe! I turned and left. Terrified by time I ran from the station. Outside were two working girls.

"Looking for some fun?" the first asked.

"But a hotel," I stammered, hoping to hide.

She led me into a dingy building. Mister Tom came down the stairs and gave me a dirty wink. "Best be quick," he sniggered.

"The back door!"

The girl took the stolen wallet. She pointed towards a door and I returned to the streets. Too much time had passed. Resigned, I walked to the city centre park and sat on an empty bench. From behind, a hand stroked my cheek in a caress; and as the hand slipped from my chin in an elegant gesture, the long claws slid from Miss Si's fingertips.

"Time's up, little mouse," she breathed into my ear.

Presumptions, image by Hazel Butler

Presumptions

Mary Dougherty

He didn't know how long he had been unconscious. All the instruments had ceased functioning when the shuttle crashed. The monitors were blank, showing him nothing of the exterior. When he decided he was not concussed, and his heartbeat had slowed to a normal rate, he ate a meal, strapped his service weapon to his survival suit, took a helmet to protect him from extremes of climate, and opened the airlock.

A forest of bright green tree trunks barred his view in all directions. The trees were tall and supple, curiously smooth-barked, and they swayed in the wind, their crowns obscuring the sky. The data processor in the helmet analysed the air and declared it breathable, gave him the air temperature and pressure, and told him of an approaching storm. He was trained not to panic, to adapt quickly to hostile surroundings. All emotions— fear, wonder, anxiety—were suppressed in the interests of survival. So when the helmet ceased functioning, and the heat inside became uncomfortable he simply took a deep breath and took it off.

Immediately he was aware of the strange air currents. Not a wind, more like a river of rippling cords, some slow and sluggish, others faster, violent, weaving a tangle of movement back and forth that bent tree trunks and buffeted him about, making progress difficult. Noises hit him from all sides, chirrupings and rustlings, and an increasing rumbling as if from the gathering storm. His scalp prickled with unease and the feeling of being watched.

The light that filtered through the far away green canopy had not changed, but he felt vibrations through the soles of his boots. He could see nothing in any direction but slender green trunks, and far overhead, snatches of bright sky.

He stalked through the vegetation like a prowling cat, all his senses alert to danger, predators, or possible prey. He stepped over roots, pushed between trunks until his eyes could take no more of the zebra-striped landscape. He turned to make his way back to the shuttle, hoping to get some of the circuits working again, to make a defendable base, a shelter from the invisible eyes.

The vibrations increased, became thudding, and the air hummed, the light dimmed. The storm, he thought, and tried to hurry. The ground shook, and the temperature dropped suddenly as shadow spread, and a hot, damp wind, carried a rank smell that made him gag. Something crashed through the vegetation before him and hit the ground, felling green trunks. He staggered, caught in the whiplash of feathery branches.

Above the broken canopy, he saw not sky, not cloud, but something dense and bristling and full of life. Broken trunks held him fast, terror-stricken as the darkness thrust itself at him, a rubbery mass glistening with damp. Fetid wind roared from a fissure beneath the twitching mass framed in quivering spikes. The fissure opened, revealing an undulating, spongy field of pink tongue and the bone-white glint of canines. He screamed. Briefly.

The Best and Last Hiss, image by Evelinn Enoksen

The Best and Last Hiss

C.N. Lesley

Borris startled awake; his last memories were of a two-leg intruder into his domain. His own beloved two-legs, Mary, screaming, her wails querulous with age while he attacked the stranger, then the agony of being smashed against a wall with his tail almost wrenched off. He must have had a nightmare.

Mary had filled his bowl with shredded hams. His mouth watered . . . nothing like eating a treat to rid his mind of a nightmare. He sauntered to his bowl on strangely light feet. But what was this? It wouldn't go in his mouth! Thoroughly ticked off, he went to find Mary, to yowl his complaint about the evil hams.

She lay on the floor, broken and covered with blood. A figure made all of rainbows rocked in a kneeling position near Mary's body. It was his

Mary outside her body. His fur bristled in outrage and fear. Borris ran for the door, a shut door, but his unnatural speed hurtled him at it, through it. He leapt in the air, spooked.

He retraced his steps, fluffing up when he slid through a solid door. But Mary wouldn't hear him. She didn't call him a brave, black boy, like when she took him to the vet's after he was hurt fighting the ginger tom. Borris caught the scent of the two-legs who had done this. It guided him down the street into a yard with high grass, ideal for hunting. Borris didn't want mice, he wanted his hams. He oozed through the door and up until he reached the top floor apartment. There was the two-leg intruder gloating over Mary's sparklies, her scent all over them. Boris puffed up to give his best hiss.

*

Jake Morrinson gloated over his haul. He thought the old woman might have a stash of cash, but never that the dried up old stick would have real jewellery. A cold breeze whistled through his living room. He started to turn when he saw it. A black panther with flattened ears and sharp fangs. Jake bounded out of his chair to the balcony, slamming the door behind him. Trembling, he reached for his cell phone to call animal control, cursing whoever it was that harboured such a beast. A growl behind him raised the hair on the back of his neck. This wasn't real. He screamed when it leapt, flying backwards, hitting the railings, falling.

*

Borris ambled over to sit on the twitching intruder's chest, determined he would be its last sight. The pained breathing ceased, a red cloud emanated from the body, to be sucked into the ground. Borris was a good boy.

Mary still knelt on the floor rocking when he sidled up to her. She picked him up, holding him close, and the rainbow washed over him until he wasn't a black cat anymore. He batted her face with his paw as they moved into the light together. Now he would have his hams.

Mourning Ritual, image by Snow Wulf

Mourning Ritual

Mike Hargreaves

The First Cat began to mourn our family's loss at midnight. It cried out into the dark skies over the city from our rooftop. And before long other cats joined it. Mangy flea bitten alley cats climbed up from the sewers and sang a screeching lament. Prissy house cats from the richest guild houses meandered down from higher roofs, deigning to join their lower cousins for this night's vigil. All the city's cats gathered here above our heads to call out to the starless sky and tell how my father had died.

Before long, neighbours came out to shush the choir of cats, eventually throwing pebbles and other debris. One stone smashed through an upper window and mother squealed in shock. My brothers went out to chase off those who would show such disrespect, but by now the crowd was too large, so they simply returned to the sanctuary of our home.

I watched from the broken window as the noise above drowned out my sorrow. I watched as the people below grew angrier. If only they could understand what had happened in this room. Surely some empathy could be shown. Our neighbours hated us, though, across the city, our bloodline was of the highest rank. We were not loved by our neighbours, that might be true, but now even the unloved deserved a measure of compassion.

Turning, I looked at the lifeless thing that had been my father. I was too young to understand what it was the shaman was doing. He had told us that father was strong and not to fear, but now he was gone. What would I do? What would any of us do?

Mother comforted me and explained. She had me count my toes on one side. This is how I learned that I would not have to mourn for father. She told me about the previous times he had been alive, and that he would live again once more. He would take me hunting again. I tried to smile.

Mother lifted me down from the window and brought me closer to the gnarly old shaman. He was intoning our ancestors to return father to us. His words seemed strange as he spoke. The shaman used the counting words, and as he moved from the eighth to the ninth my father's body twitched. All his hair stood on end and slowly he was standing again on all fours, alive.

The First Cat came to us in all his glory. My father thanked him for his patronage. We heard the mews and purrs of the other city cats as they ended their banshee like role in the ritual.

I looked again at my toes: five on each of my front paws and four on my back two paws. Counting them on either side gave me nine. Mother said we all have nine lives. But only the most fortunate will be allowed to live them all. I hope I am among the fortunate cats that do.

The Secret Life of Walter Kitty, image by Lienne

The Secret Life of Walter Kitty

Tina Closser

The orange tabby cat soared through the sky on his faithful reptilian steed. The wind whipped through his fur, chilling him, yet sending the feeling of freedom through his being. Below he could see tiny houses through the patchwork of clouds. The glistening blue dragon pitched and yawed, and the orange tabby's body followed every movement.

From a distance, he heard, "Help me! Someone please help me!"

The dragon turned his head. "So, Mr. Walter, should we see what's going on?"

Walter smiled. "I wouldn't have it any other way, Rygar."

Rygar spiraled toward the ground; Walter always hated it when he showed off like that. Rygar stretched his wings out wide, and they glided to the ground like a leaf on the wind.

In front of them, they saw a quivering black puppy looking up at a large snarling Dobermann. Walter hissed, and his fur puffed. "What kind of foul rapscallion would threaten such a small helpless scamp?"

The Dobermann snarled and barked, but Walter stood steadfast. "Mind your own business. All the pup needs to do is hand over the treats, and no one will get hurt."

The puppy whined and sniffed, "Please, Mr. Dobermann these treats are all I have to feed my sick mother and litter mates. I've gone long and far to find these treats. I must deliver them home; my family is counting on me."

The Dobermann gave a cruel laugh. "Tell someone who cares. Hand them over or forfeit your life."

Walter unsheathed his sword. "Back you foul heathen! Pick on someone your own size!"

The Dobermann turned from the pup and licked his chops. "Are you offering yourself, kitty?"

"With pleasure!"

The Dobermann looked Walter up and down and in an instant lunged. Walter held out his sword and pierced the snarling canine in the shoulder. Dobermann shrieked and jumped back. "You'll regret that, Walter."

"Give me your best shot!"

The canine inspected his wounds then lunged for Walter, knocking him to the ground and his sword from his hand. In two tail wags, Dobermann had Walter pinned. When he spoke his hot damp breath moistened Walter's fur. "I have you pinned. What are you going to do now?"

Walter thought a moment then turned and bit one of the massive canine's paws.

Then there was a thud on Walter's head; he blinked his eyes and looked up. He was no longer in the grassy meadow but on the food-provider's lap. She shook her pink paw, then said, "Bad, kitty. You were sleep biting again." The food-provider placed him on the floor. "If you're going to act like that, then sleep somewhere else."

Walter found his favorite sunbeam and closed his eyes. Within a few seconds, a dusty landscape surrounded him, and he was riding his trusty white stallion. Numerous cacti passed him by. It was hot, too hot. As he took a drink from his canteen to quench his parched throat, he heard a cry . . .

The Clockwork Cat Escapes

Kieran Mathers

George opened the door of the cage, and the clockwork cat shied back from his hand as he reached to gingerly pet the automaton.

He and Professor Herbert Johns-Wirtely had both been working hard on their feline masterpiece for the last few months. The Professor was hoping that, as a noted ailurophile, Queen Victoria would pay special attention to this automaton. His master had often espoused what the benefits of royal patronage would do for both of their prospects.

So as the cat was to be presented tomorrow, Georgie decided to check the springs which powered the creature. He'd already finished his day's chores; the laboratory was now as clean and as tidy as it could be. The Professor was particularly keen on this, severely disliking any dirt or mess.

As the cat cowered, the low throbbing of Zeppelin rotors shaking the room distracted Georgie. It must be the nine thirty Berlin Zeppelin, but why was it so strangely low? At that moment, the cat took its opportunity and leapt past him, through the open cage door and into the laboratory.

"Damnation!" Georgie swore as the cat flew past, landing on the other side of the room by the dark oak bookcases. He raised his hands in what he hoped was a non-threatening gesture and went after it while the little automaton preened its golden bronzed surface with a cast silver tongue.

"Here, clockwork kitty," he muttered, and then dived forward to grab the machine.

It leapt out of the way, slipping his grasp, and he crashed to the floor with a thump. Georgie would've sworn he got a finger to it, but the cat had escaped him with ease. It meowed at him, reproachfully, its expressionless glass eyes still somehow mocking. Then, with a flick of its tail, the cat slipped easily beneath the metal and glass shape of the aether generator.

Straining, Georgie tried to reach but the cat kept shying away from his hand. After waiting until his arm was up to his shoulder beneath this device, the cat then easily slipped away, climbing effortlessly onto the generator's embossed dome. It gave him another smug look.

Georgie scowled and stood up, his shirt-sleeve now hopelessly filthy. The cat then leapt to the table, upsetting the test tubes carefully laid out there. Georgie grabbed for it and missed again. It leapt to the bookcase and, in a remarkable tornado of destruction, dislodged dozens of books. Climbing the shelves gingerly, he tried to grab the cat with one hand, but he couldn't quite reach and fell instead, landing hard on his back. Another book hit him as he lay, stunned.

As it leapt from the bookcase his hand shot out and he finally caught the cat's segmented tail.

"Got you!" Georgie's voice was venomous. The cat hung helpless like a hooked fish, mewling pathetically.

At that moment, the Professor pushed open the laboratory door. A carefully arched eyebrow told Georgie just how much trouble he was in.

I Am Still Here, image by Evelinn Enoksen

I Am Still Here

Evelinn Enoksen

When sadness fills her face, I
wish I could take her place,
so she would know I'm still here.

She was my love, she had my soul,
my body, my mind and my life.
She was my darling wife.

I am not what I once was,
but she still has the things I've given her,
and she still remembers the cause.
Our home is the same as always,
perhaps because I'm still there.
Perhaps my presence lingers in the air.

She did not shed a tear at my funeral,
but her heart was filled with salty water,

as she embraced our loving daughter.

They say I have nine lives,
and in a way they're right.
I remember all my former lives well.
I was a flower, I was a tree,
I was a hawk and a bee.
I was a bear, I was a worm,
and even a hare.

Then I was a human,
We were together, we were apart,
but when I died, I broke her heart.

I still get to enjoy many moments
curled up in her lap,
Listening to our music and her
feet go tap – tap – tap.
But now I don't walk, I saunter.
Instead of talking, I purr.
Though it must be said,
I was furry as a human too,
except for on my head.
Now the nights are long, I hunt
and mate and sing my song.
I jump, I climb. I never fall.
My nature hasn't changed at all.

Sometimes she reads me stories I
know well, stories we shared,
stories I used to tell.
When sadness fills her face, I
wish I could take her place,
so she would know I'm still here.

I am here, I am here, and there is nothing to fear.
If only she could see, if only I
could be the eighth me.
We have this last moment to share,
if only she could know that I am still here.

The Door, image by A.F.E Smith

The Door

Selina Carr

The humans are always complaining. Let the cat in, let the cat out, let the cat in again. Think they're so smart with their thumbs. But today the big one is doing something to the door. It's very noisy and there's a lot of dust. I don't like dust—at least not in the air. On the ground it's nice to roll in. Good for the fur. Stupid humans think you need water to have good fur. Water, of all things! Idiots.

They laugh at my sneezes, like there's something funny about my lungs filling with dust. I sneezed so hard a moment ago I almost fell off the sofa. They stopped laughing when they saw what my claws did to the upholstery. Serves them right.

Now they're all grinning at me like dogs, expecting something. *What? What do you want? Stop looking at me!* I roll on my back. *If you're going to stand there, you might as well do something useful. Rub my belly.*

They're not rubbing my belly. It's as if they have one brain between the four of them. The big one looks particularly proud for someone who doesn't even have a tail.

"Come on, Squiggle, get off your bum and see what Daddy's made you," says the soft one. I trust her only slightly more than the others. Bringer of kibble. I yawn and wash my face. Let them wait.

The smallest one, the one I still haven't forgiven for pulling my tail all those times, even though it's bigger now and wants to be my friend, comes over to me, its arms out as if it will pick me up. I dodge left at the last minute and stroll over to the door. They exchange excited glances and follow me, creeping along as if they know how to stalk. Please. They couldn't catch a cold.

But what's this? A window has been cut into the door right at my level. The sun is shining in the garden, the birds fat and dancing in the stone bird bath. Is this some sort of joke? Do they want to torture me further by letting me see the outside only they can give me access to? Cretins.

"It's a door, silly," the small one says, and leans down to flick at the window with its stubby fingers.

Miraculously, the window swings open and a gust of cool air tickles my whiskers. Delicious.

"Now you can go in and out whenever you want!" It claps its fleshy palms together, making my fur stand on end. I hate that.

Ignoring their trills of pleasure, I push a paw at the window. It's light, and swings easily at my touch, the air outside hot and damp this time. *Damp!* I shudder and draw my paw inside. I sit and wash my face a moment, enjoying their disappointment. Eventually, the soft one convinces them to leave me be. The big one mutters something about ungrateful wretches.

When they're gone, I push with my head, opening the window all the way. It's dark outside, and fresh. Mice scamper everywhere, and a flash of slanting green eyes and the swish of a soft tail coaxes me out. Not a human in sight. Yes, this is the world in which I shall take my first adventure.

One-Eye, image by Evelinn Enoksen

One Eye

Joel Cornah

She could jump; the human world would vanish, and she could be anywhere. One-Eye had seen ten thousand worlds and ten thousand years - she had been in worlds where the sky had been filled with fire, and she had been in worlds where there had been no sky at all.

To jump cost her, though. At first it had been small - a hair of fur, a lump of fat - she'd not given it much thought until she'd jumped to the land of sand and dust with half a tail. She'd stayed there for years, rallying the cats, fooling herself into believing she was doing something important.

"I'll leave when my brothers and sisters are treated like gods," she had said over and over. But it had taken nearly a century, and no matter how many pyramids or temples had been built, she had not moved.

She had been frightened. One-Eye, who had seen the Shadow of Time, who had walked across galaxies and spoken with beings beyond human comprehension; One-Eye had been afraid.

The others had seen it and had plotted against her. She'd been in her temple, curled on a pillow of silk, surrounded by humans with wafting fans. But the other cats had hissed, had showed their claws and challenged her. Day followed day, and the attacks had grown in frequency and ferocity. They'd once called her their Queen, and then they'd called her a demon.

Perhaps that's what she was. She had never met a cat who could jump like she could; she had never met another cat who could sing the song of space, or hear the sound of eternity. One-Eye was unique; she was alone.

She had left the land of sand and dust when they'd ambushed her in the night. She'd been rolling with the great ginger monstrosity who had been pretender to her throne. They'd scratched and bitten one another, but the ginger was big, powerful, and young. One-Eye had jumped to a world of ice and snow; ginger had been dragged with her, though, and wailed in the cold. One-Eye had left her there and jumped again.

So many years had passed since then; a deluge of time that left her bones feeling like the sand she had once trodden. She hadn't jumped in over a decade; the last one had cost her an eye. Half-blind and old - old beyond the count of cat or human - she had confined herself to the human world once more. And now she sat in a cold, white room, weighing her own fate in her mind.

She knew what was in the syringe - she knew what the humans' words meant.

"She's ill, she's old, and it's for the best."

Old, yes, if only they knew. But ill? No, she was not ill. And yet, she wondered - she wondered what it might be like to enter oblivion. The moment would come soon, and she would have to make her choice. Stay or go. She could jump and risk losing another eye, or worse. Or she could stay and sleep - sleep forever. She'd been awake forever; she could not recall ever having been a kitten, she could not remember a family. There was just time, endless time beyond count.

The needle was in, the warmth spreading through her leg. She raised her remaining eye and looked the white-clad human in the face.

"I'm tired," she said. The human's expression was a mixture of shock and horror, but One-Eye didn't care. It was over. Centuries of jumping, of leading, of running; it was time to sleep at long last.

About the Authors

A.F.E SMITH is an academic editor who lives in the south east of England with her husband, her young son, and thousands of books. When she's not writing speculative fiction of various kinds, she enjoys the usual things: watching films, eating snacks, solving complex mathematical equations. She has never owned a cat, mainly because she knows she'd end up a pawn in its bid for world domination.

C.N LESLEY lives in Alberta with her husband and cats. Her three daughters live close by. When she isn't writing, Elizabeth likes to read and to paint watercolors. She is also a keen gardener, despite the very short summers and now has a mature shade garden. Once a worker in the communications sector, mostly concentrating on local news and events, she now writes full time.

RACHAEL BROWN is a fourteen-year-old student from Norfolk. Her interests include art, animation, gaming, history, reading, seventies rock music, drama, and of course writing. She is intensely passionate about English and writing, and thinks it is a real pleasure to be included in this anthology, especially since her stories (whether short or long) tend to be rather bizarre and odd with a zany feel.

PAIGE CLOSSER attends school in small town in the American Midwest. She loves to read Percy Jackson novels and make loom band charms. When she's not busy with those pursuits, or practicing violin, she likes to think of stories. The story in this book may or may not be based on her two cats.

CHRISTIE RAMPERSAD is a medical student who began her writing in poetry, with selected works appearing in *Danse Macabre* and *Pens on Fire*. Now, as she transitions to fiction, she is thrilled that *Nine Lives Later* has placed joint-third in the Kristell Ink Feline Flash Fiction Competition and found a home in this anthology.

DAVE CROSBY is an affable gentleman, as much as any American can be "affable" (or "gentle", for that matter), living in a Heaven-forsaken area of California known as Fresno. He has a humanities heart and mind, living in an ex-banker's body, so he has made a living with bankerly number-crunching all his life, but has lived with reading, writing and music. He published a short story in 2013, *Rain Over Ghaidhealtachd*, set in Ancient Scotland, in the anthology *Magic Creatures from Celtic Mists*, has written another tale set within a moonlit night in Jamaica, *Last Touch*, and hopes to publish his first novel next year, an exciting thriller set in San Francisco, called *Bringing Home the Good War*. He thinks kindly of his two sons, Glen and Ted, who have given him much inspiration in his work, especially the novel.

JESSICA FROST is a medical student with a love for literature. For her, writing is a much-needed break away from science and studying! She can be found on Twitter: @ MissInkweaver

CLAIRE NEILSON was always very good at stories in school, but her spelling was awful. She thanks the gods and goddesses of word processors for the little red lines of spelling correction. Now age 30 she lives in Manchester and spends her days baking for a living and reading for leisure.

BRIAN TALGO was born in the Deep South of the US in 1954, and later spent his formative years in Westchester County, a northern suburb of New York City. As a young man he wandered restlessly about the US for several years, working mainly as a carpenter and stonemason, until he eventually got in touch with his inner Viking and relocated to Norway in 1981. After many years abroad he has grown comfortable with his expat status.

Currently working with international admissions at the University of Oslo, Brian writes and indulges in other creative endeavors in his spare time. He presently lives on the outskirts of Oslo, together with his wife, son, two insubordinate cats, and a miniature forest of plants. A daughter has wisely flown the coop.

Website: sonsrevenge.blogspot.no

IAN RICHARDSON lives by the sea, on the East Coast of Scotland, with his cat, Purry Murray.

The first story Ian ever wrote was published, but he hasn't been able to keep up that 100% record. However, several short stories, articles and micro fictions have escaped the red pen recently and his steampunk serial was e-published in 2013.

ROB BAYLISS lives with his wife, two children and dog in Somerset. A keen scholar of history and lover of fantasy, only recently has he discovered the joyful escapism of sitting down to write a story.

LANCE CROSS writes short stories when he gets stuck writing his novel, so he writes more short stories than he should.

When he's not writing, he spends too much time telling his cat he's "sooooo cute", and trying to keep him away from the computer keyboard, as he knows what buttons to push to delete stuff. Lance really shouldn't let him jump on the desk in the first place, but as mentioned, he's sooooo cute.

JOSHUA CORNAH is a 22 year old café assistant at a local coffee shop who loves to draw, for himself and others. In his free time, he's an illustrator and cartoonist, and the influences for his drawings come from Japanese anime, manga, and Nintendo video games. He is also very polite.

STEVEN J GUSCOTT or Steven, Steve, Steve-o, Stevie, Stevie Gee, Moral Steve, Uncle Steven . . . the list goes on . . . but the name he has chosen for writing is Steven J. Guscott. Like some of the other names, there's a random story behind it, and obviously his middle name starts with a J, but he's not going to bore you with that story just now. What he will bore you with is telling you how much he loves creating fantasy/sci fi stories. He's twenty six and lives in Scotland, and nearly three years ago he discovered an unhealthy obsession with writing. He's written a few stories in this time, and has quite a number still to write. If you want to learn more about Steven and his writing journey, he's kept a record in the form of a blog that can be found at:

www.stevenjguscott.co.uk

VICTORIA ROBINSON lives a safe and comfortable existence in home county suburbia, where shadows lurk not in dark, smoking alleys but behind neatly trimmed hedges and carefully erected fences.

DAVID COHEN lives in the university town of Dunedin, a gateway to New Zealand's Lord-of-the-Rings-set Southern landscapes. His background is in the high-technology electronic industries, but considers writing the most fun you can have sitting down with a pen and paper, so is pursuing that – as well as other interests such as photography, object-making and volunteer work for Habitat for Humanity. He cites Annie Proulx, Spike Milligan, Arthur C. Clarke, Patrick Süskind, and Terry Pratchett as current influences, but that will almost certainly change.

HONOR THOMPSON spends most of her time with her head in a book and a pen in her hand. She looks to her friends and family for inspiration, and as such all her writing characters hold a special place in her heart. Without her grandparents, she wouldn't be where she is today, for they taught her that nothing is impossible; you just have to believe.

SOPHIE TALLIS is a Bristol born gal who grew up in a sleepy village dreaming of dragons and wild adventures. She hasn't grown up much, and sincerely hopes she never does. She lives in the Cotswolds with her family, two enormous white wolves, and a load of wild ducks that basically run the place; she has just added two Alaskan Malamutes into the mix! Sophie is a full-time teacher and has been dulling young minds . . . ahem . . . inspiring young minds for the past fifteen years. She is a painter, artist and illustrator, and has a BA (Hons) Degree in Fine Art, photography and sculpture. But her first passion has always been writing stories and poetry. Her first novel, an epic fantasy for children and adults, was published in September 2012 to great reviews and high sales, and she's currently working on the sequels, due out later in 2014 and 2015, as well as a host of other projects.

WILL MACMILLAN-JONES is a fifty-something lover of blues, rock and jazz. He presently lives in Wales, a beautiful verdant land of myth with a rich cultural heritage. He does his best to support this heritage by drinking local beers and shouting loud encouragement at the TV whenever Wales is playing international rugby.

He has just fulfilled a lifetime ambition by filling an entire wall of his study with bookcases, and then (over)filling the bookcases. When not drinking beer and watching rugby, he remembers to write the occasional horror book or to add to his comic fantasy series, *The Banned Underground*. Links to all his work can be found on his website:

www.willmacmillanjones.com

JANE DOUGHTERY is a product of the Irish diaspora. She was brought up in Yorkshire, educated at Manchester and London, then moved to Paris to work in the wine trade. She now lives in Bordeaux with her family, a Spanish greyhound, and a posse of cats. Her first published work is a YA fantasy series, *The Green Woman*. She also writes poetry and has been published in *Poetry Nook Magazine* and *The Bamboo Hut*.

As a Role Player, **MIKE HARGREAVES'** main outlet for creative writing is in the plotting out of tabletop gaming scenarios for the RPG players in his social circle. The rest of the time he's fighting to keep a healthy ratio between ideas and completed projects. It's a fight he keeps losing.

When she isn't busy with her nine-to-five job as an electrical engineer, **TINA CLOSSER** helps her husband with a small hobby farm, complete with a mini horse, donkey, cows, and sheep. In between farm duties and running the kids to gymnastics, she likes to write.

KIERAN MATHERS is a freelance writer based in Sheffield, UK, and is very much inspired by *A Song of Ice and Fire, The Farseer Trilogy* and other great works of fantasy. While not hunched over a keyboard creating worlds in his head, he goes cycling in the Yorkshire Dales and writes poetry.

EVELINN ENOKSEN lives in Norway with her husband and children. She finds inspiration in everything, and has always been interested in art and writing. She says there are few things more fun in life than being able to create.

SELINA CARR is a writer, collector and lover of folk and fairy tales. She is inspired by, and drawn to, the deceptive simplicity of these sometimes poignant—and often gruesome—stories. Much of her writing is heavily influenced by her life-long relationship with the tales penned by the Brothers Grimm, Hans Christian Andersen, Charles Perrault and Oscar Wilde.

JOEL CORNAH hailing from a small isolated village in Lancashire, is the author responsible for *The Sea-Stone Sword*. He was awarded a degree in Creative Writing from Liverpool John Moors University and spent seven years writing a comical newspaper for *The Barrow Downs* Tolkien discussion forum. Accompanying this paper was a comic strip series called *The Phantom and Alien*, a bizarre story of bus drivers, dead people, and a slime child bent on inconveniencing everyone around him.

Facebook: www.facebook.com/JoelKCornah

Grimbold Kristell Inklings

6259531R00073

Printed in Great Britain
by Amazon.co.uk, Ltd.,
Marston Gate.